Extreme Sports

BMX

Rebecca Koehn

DiscoverRoo
An Imprint of Pop!
popbooksonline.com

abdobooks.com

Published by Pop!, a division of ABDO, PO Box 398166, Minneapolis, Minnesota 55439.

Printed in the United States of America, North Mankato, Minnesota.

052020
092020

THIS BOOK CONTAINS RECYCLED MATERIALS

Cover Photo: iStockphoto
Interior Photos: iStockphoto, 1, 13, 20, 22, 29; Shutterstock Images, 5, 6, 7, 8–9, 14, 17, 18, 19, 21, 23, 27, 30, 31; Schwinn/Getty Images News/Getty Images, 11; Tony Donaldson/Icon SMI 558/Newscom, 15; Kyodo/AP Images, 25; Oleg Zabielin/Alamy, 28

Editor: Brienna Rossiter
Series Designer: Jake Slavik

Library of Congress Control Number: 2019954954

Publisher's Cataloging-in-Publication Data

Names: Koehn, Rebecca, author.

Title: BMX / by Rebecca Koehn

Description: Minneapolis, Minnesota : POP!, 2021 | Series: Extreme sports | Includes online resources and index.

Identifiers: ISBN 9781532167812 (lib. bdg.) | ISBN 9781532168918 (ebook)

Subjects: LCSH: BMX freestyle (Stunt cycling)--Juvenile literature. | Stunt cycling--Juvenile literature. | BMX bikes--Juvenile literature. | Extreme sports--Juvenile literature. | Sports--Juvenile literature.

Classification: DDC 796.046--dc23

WELCOME TO DiscoverRoo!

Pop open this book and you'll find QR codes loaded with information, so you can learn even more!

Scan this code* and others like it while you read, or visit the website below to make this book pop!

popbooksonline.com/bmx

*Scanning QR codes requires a web-enabled smart device with a QR code reader app and a camera.

TABLE OF CONTENTS

CHAPTER 1

PEDAL POWER

Eight BMX racers line up behind the starting gate. A buzzer sounds. The riders plunge down a 26-foot (7.9-m) slope. Their bikes go from 0 to 35 miles per hour (0–56 km/h) in just two seconds.

WATCH A VIDEO HERE!

The starting gate keeps bikes at the top of the slope until the race begins.

At a BMX track, the corners have raised sides called berms.

The racers speed around the first turn. They sprint down a **straightaway**. Then they hit the first **obstacle**. It's a double, or two hills in a row. The riders fly up the first slope. They sail over both hills and land on the other side.

Leaning forward helps riders balance and steer.

At competitions, riders take turns racing around the track in small groups.

The next obstacle is a step-down. This is a tall hill followed by a shorter hill. Riders pedal hard down both hills to gain speed. This speed sends them flying off the jump that follows. The riders land and keep pedaling. Then they race toward the finish line.

DID YOU KNOW?

Most BMX races last only 25 to 40 seconds.

CHAPTER 2

KID CREATED

BMX is short for "bicycling **motocross**." Kids in California created the sport in the 1960s. At that time, motocross racing was popular in the United States. In this sport,

LEARN MORE HERE!

Kids ride their bikes around their neighborhood in the 1960s.

people race motorcycles called dirt bikes on rough tracks.

Kids pretended their bicycles were dirt bikes. They raced their friends. In the early 1970s, a movie about motorcycles included a clip of kids riding BMX bikes. The kids went off jumps and did tricks. Many viewers decided to try BMX too. The sport took off.

DID YOU KNOW?

The first BMX race took place in 1969.

BMX BIKE PARTS

SMALL AND STURDY

BMX bikes have smaller wheels than other bicycles. The small wheels keep riders closer to the ground. This gives riders better control for landing jumps and doing tricks. BMX bikes also have small seats. Racers only sit before and after a race. During the race, they stand on the pedals.

The wheels of a BMX bike are often 20 inches (51 cm) wide.

By the 1980s, there were BMX events and **competitions** around the world. Companies began to make bikes just for the sport.

Dave Mirra competes at the X Games in 1998.

CHAPTER 3

RACING AND TRICKING

There are two main types of BMX events. The first is BMX racing. This sport takes place on dirt tracks. The tracks are 900 to 1,100 feet (274–335 m) long. They can

LEARN MORE HERE!

BMX races are held all year round.

be indoors or outdoors. Each track has a different set of **obstacles**.

Rollers often come in rows of two to four.

Racers ride through the obstacles to reach the finish line. Many tracks have rollers. Racers bounce over these small hills. Tabletops are also common. These jumps have flat tops. Racers sometimes do small tricks or **poses** in the air as they go over them.

Many tricks involve tilting or spinning the handlebars.

Ramps launch BMX riders into the air to do tricks.

The second type of BMX is freestyle. It is all about tricks. Riders use ramps and other obstacles to get air. They often ride in **halfpipes** or skate parks. In freestyle **competitions**, riders perform for a group of judges. The judges give each rider a score. Riders get more points for harder tricks.

Advanced riders can swing their bikes around before landing.

Beginners start by learning wheelies and bunny hops. In a wheelie, the front tire tips up into the air. For a bunny hop, both wheels lift off the ground. Harder tricks include flips and spins. A half-circle spin is called a 180. A full spin is a 360.

A BMX rider does a wheelie at a competition in Russia.

A freestyle rider flies off a vert ramp to do a flip. Vert ramps have tall, steep sides.

DID YOU KNOW?

Expert riders can do two complete spins in the air. This trick is called a 720.

SUPERSTAR

HANNAH ROBERTS

- Hannah Roberts began BMX biking when she was 9 years old.
- She entered her first competition in 2012. By age 16, she was one of the best BMX freestyle riders in the world.
- In 2017, Roberts was BMX Freestyle World Champion. She got the bronze medal in 2018. She won first place again in 2019.
- Roberts practices 40 hours every week at a skate park. She also teaches young riders.

Hannah Roberts competes at the Urban Cycling World Championships in 2019.

- Roberts was a member of the National Honor Society at her high school. Even with all the time she spent practicing, she kept her grades up.

CHAPTER 4

SAFETY FIRST

BMX biking can be dangerous. Riders can crash or fall. So, most events require riders to wear protective gear. For BMX racing, all riders must wear helmets. They must wear long-sleeved shirts and long

COMPLETE AN ACTIVITY HERE!

Bright-colored gear helps fans spot their favorite riders.

pants as well. This clothing protects their arms and legs if they wipe out, or crash.

For freestyle events, riders must wear helmets, elbow pads, and knee pads. Riders can add more safety gear if they want. For example, they often wear goggles and gloves.

Helmets for BMX freestyle are smaller than racing helmets.

DID YOU KNOW?

A rider's shirt is called a jersey.

Riders practice their stunts in São Paolo, Brazil, in 2017.

MAKING CONNECTIONS

TEXT-TO-SELF

Would you rather try BMX racing or freestyle? Why would you choose that type of event?

TEXT-TO-TEXT

What other books about extreme sports have you read? How are those sports similar to or different from BMX?

TEXT-TO-WORLD

BMX riders start with small tricks before learning harder ones. What are some other activities that require practice?

GLOSSARY

competition – an event where a person's skills are compared to other people's skills.

halfpipe – a U-shaped ramp. Athletes move up and down the ramp's sides to do tricks.

motocross – motorcycle racing that involves riding dirt bikes around dirt tracks filled with obstacles.

obstacle – something that blocks the way.

pose – a way of holding the body in a certain position.

straightaway – a straight section of a racetrack.

INDEX

ONLINE RESOURCES

popbooksonline.com

Scan this code* and others like it while you read, or visit the website below to make this book pop!

popbooksonline.com/bmx

*Scanning QR codes requires a web-enabled smart device with a QR code reader app and a camera.